# THE
# SMALL POTATOES
# CLUB

**Harriet Ziefert**

**Illustrated by Richard Brown**

A Young Yearling Book

Lewis

Published by
Dell Publishing
a division of
Bantam Doubleday Dell Publishing Group, Inc.
666 Fifth Avenue
New York, New York 10103

ISBN: 0-440-48034-5

Printed in the United States of America

April 1984

10 9 8 7 6 5

CWO

*For Jamie,*
*my smallest potato*

# CHAPTER ONE

# THE GANG

Hi. We're a group.
We're friends.
We stick together.
If you stick with us, you'll have
a good time.

I'll introduce you to everybody.
There's Roger, Sam, Chris,
Molly, Sue, Scott, and Spot.
Roger wears glasses.
Sam has freckles.
Chris is tall and Molly is not.
Sue has braids and Scott does not.
And Spot is Spot. (He's also Molly's dog.)

Sometimes we play ball.

We play until everyone starts arguing.

Then we have to think of something else to do.

Sometimes we have races.

When Molly is last, Sue shouts, "Hurry up!"

And Molly answers, "But I'm running as fast
as I can!"

Sometimes we play follow-the-leader.
Sue likes to be leader and Sam does not.

"Follow me and do what I do!" shouts Sue. "That's what you always say," complains Sam. "You're too bossy!"

One day someone had a really great idea.

"Let's start a club and build a clubhouse."

Sam thinks it was his idea.

But Molly says it was hers.

Sam and Molly argued until someone said,
"Stop arguing and let's get started."

Sue said, "We need rope and string—some
sheets and blankets too!"

"Is that all we need?" asked Chris.

"No," said Sam. "We'll also need branches
to make a roof."

"I know where to find two big branches," said
Scott. "Who'll help me carry them?"

"I will," said Molly.

*"Arf! Arf!"* barked Spot.

"I'll go ask my mother for some rope," said
Roger.

"Me too," said Chris. "We'll need a lot of rope."

"And we'll ask for sheets and blankets," said
Sue and Sam.

"Hurry, everybody! Be back here with the stuff in twenty minutes," yelled Molly.

# CHAPTER TWO

# BUILDING A CLUBHOUSE

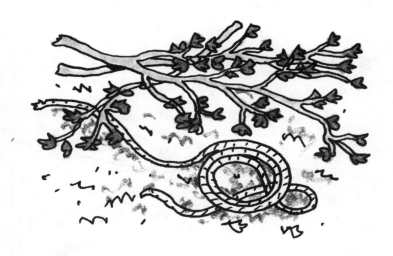

"Let's get going," said Molly. "We have
   to tie a rope between the trees."
Molly stood near one tree.
Sam stood near another.
"This is not easy," said Sam.
"Nothing's easy," said Chris, "but we can
   do it!"

Three more ropes had to be tied around trees.

Scott and Roger helped with the tying.

When they were pulled tight, the ropes formed
a square.

"Now we're ready to hang the blankets," said
  Chris. "If we use two blankets in the
  front, we'll have a door."

"Spot, get out of the way," said Molly. "If
  you don't move, you'll be stepped on."

"Get the roof branches," yelled Molly.

"And watch what you're doing!"

Molly, Sam, and Roger put the roof branches
in place.

"Boy, what a neat roof," said Sam. "It lets
the light in."

"And the rain too!" grumbled Roger.

"So what!" answered Sam.

13

The clubhouse was finished.

It looked pretty good.

"All we need is a sign," said Sue.

"What shall we write on it?" asked Sam.

"Silly question," said Sue. "We should write the name of our club!"

"Well, what's the name?" asked Scott.

Everybody started to think.

But no one spoke up.

Finally Roger said, "I think I have a
   really good idea. We should call our
   club the SMALL POTATOES. Does
   anybody know the potato rhyme?"
"Do you mean 'One potato, two potato,
   three potato, four . . .'?" asked Sue.

"That's what I mean," said Roger. "Everybody
    take a turn at being a potato. I'll start.
    I'm one potato!"
"Two potato!" said Sam.
"Three potato," said Chris.
"Four potato," said Molly.
"Five potato," said Sue.
"Six potato," said Scott.
*"Arf! Arf!"* said Spot.

"We're seven potatoes, including Spot," said
  Roger.
"Seven potatoes—that's our small gang," Molly
  shouted.
"Are any more potatoes allowed?" asked Chris.
"No more potatoes," said Roger, "at least not
  for now!"

# CHAPTER THREE

# THE GANG VOTES

Here we are. All of us.

Today we're having a meeting.

"Let's vote," said Chris.

"Yesses stand up and nos stay down,"
said Molly.

Chris looked around and counted.

"There are four yesses and three
nos—plus one *arf-arf*!"

"But what did we vote for?" asked Sue.

No one knew the answer to Sue's question.

Then someone said, "Let's vote about whether
or not we should play soccer. Yesses
stand up and nos stay down."

Again Chris looked around and counted.

"There are five yesses and two nos—
plus one bow-wow!"

"So let's play," said Sam.

"I want to be the captain of one team," said
  Sue.

"You're too bossy," said Chris.

  Sue answered, "If you want, you can be the
    captain of the other team, but I called
    it first!"

"Let's stop arguing and start playing," said
  Scott.

  So we divided up into teams.

The game started.

Sam kicked from the center.

Chris got the ball and began dribbling
toward the other team's goal.

"Kick the ball—kick it hard to me!" shouted
Molly, who loved to win.

Chris tried to pass to Molly, but
Scott stole the ball.
Scott tried to kick to Sue, but
the ball went out-of-bounds.
Chris got a throw-in.
Then Molly scored a goal.

The ball was back in the center.

Sam kicked—and guess who got
the ball?

You're right! It was Spot!

"Get out of the way, Spot!" yelled Scott.

"Stupid dog!" shouted Sam.

But all the shouting didn't help one bit.

Spot had the ball and he wouldn't let it go.

Spot sat in the middle of the field.

He smiled. He looked very happy.

We all looked at him and couldn't help
smiling back.
Someone said, "It's all right, Spot. We
    still love you!"
Molly gave Spot a pat on the head.
Then Chris said, "I guess our soccer game is
    over for today. Let's do something else."

# CHAPTER FOUR

## TO THE MUSEUM

"What are we going to do?" asked Roger.

"Let's go to the zoo," said Sue.

"Too far!" said Sam.

"I agree," said Molly. "How about the museum?"

"Now, that's a really good idea!" said Roger.

"How are we going to get there?" asked Scott.

Chris answered, "We can walk. The museum's just on the other side of the park."

"Okay," said Molly.

"*Arf, Arf,*" said Spot. He also wanted to walk.

"I don't really feel like walking," said Sam.

"Neither do I," said Roger. "Anyway, I have my bike."

"I have mine too," said Sam, "so I'll ride with you."

"Everyone who's walking—let's go," said
    Molly. "We'll meet the rest of you there."
"Riding has got to be faster than walking,"
    said Roger. "We'll *beat* you there!"
"Don't be so sure," said Scott.
"I know we can beat you there," shouted Sam
    as he pedaled down the path.
"Let's run," shouted Chris.
"Wait," said Molly. "We can take the shortcut
    through the trees. Spot knows the way."

Chris, Molly, Sue, Scott, and Spot—
all of them started walking.
Before they went too far, Sue said, "I
     have to go home to do something. I'll
     meet you in front of the museum."
After she had gone, Spot started to run.
Chris, Molly, and Scott ran behind him.
Spot was hard to keep up with.
Molly yelled to him a couple of times:
     "Slow down, Spot, you're going too fast!"

Roger and Sam were pedaling hard.

Roger was in the lead.

He was sure he was going to get to the museum before the rest of the gang.

Suddenly Roger heard Sam shout.

He looked back and saw that Sam was stuck.

Roger wanted to keep on going, but he knew Sam needed help.

Roger biked back to where Sam was. "What's the matter?" he asked.

"My pants got stuck in the chain," said Sam.

"I'll help you get unstuck," said Roger.

Sam and Roger worked together.

They were able to pull the pants from the chain.

Soon the two of them were on their way again.

Chris, Molly, Scott, and Spot were standing
in front of the museum when Roger and
Sam arrived.

Roger said, ''We would have beaten you, but
Sam's pants got stuck in his chain.''

''Too bad!'' said Molly.

''Now we can go inside,'' said Chris.

''But where's Sue?'' asked Sam.

''We have to wait for her,'' said Chris.

They waited and waited.

Finally Sue came.

Then everybody walked up the wide steps
to the entrance of the museum.

There was a big sign near the front door.

The sign said NO DOGS ALLOWED.

"Oh, no," said Roger. "What are we going to
      do with Spot?"
"Don't worry," said Molly. "I'll talk to him."
Molly bent down and whispered into Spot's ear.
Spot's tail drooped, his ears sagged, then
he walked away.

# CHAPTER FIVE

# IN THE MUSEUM

As we walked inside, we got buttons
to pin on our shirts.

"I like this button," said Scott. "It
makes me feel like I belong."

"Where should we go first?" asked Scott.

"I'd like to see the knights," said Chris.

"I'd rather see the dinosaurs," said Molly.

"But I want to see the blue whale," said Sam.

"We'll never see anything if the three of you keep on talking," said Scott. "Anyway, we're a club and I think we should stick together."

"Okay," said Molly, "let's see the knights first." Everyone agreed.

Chris asked a guard where the knights were.

The guard said, "Just take the elevator to the second floor. You'll see a model of a knight as soon as you get off."

The elevator was pretty empty.

We all rode together.

As soon as the elevator doors opened, we saw the knight.

There it was—seated on a horse and dressed in silver armor.

The horse was wearing armor too!

We walked around the knight room.

We saw swords and shields.

Chris pointed to a shield and said, "Those are coats of arms. I read a book about knights. I know all about this stuff."

"Look at that helmet," said Molly. "How could anyone see out of those slits!"

"And how could anyone move with this armor on?" asked Scott. "It must weigh a ton!"

"You can read my book," said Chris. "It explains everything."

"Now can we see the dinosaurs?" asked Molly.

"Okay," said Chris, "let's go."

In the dinosaur room there were all kinds of models.

"What's this?" asked Scott.

"Oh, that's a brontosaurus's footprint," said Roger.

"And what's this?" asked Sam.

"That must be a Tyrannosaurus Rex. I'm sure I'm right, because of the teeth," said Molly.

"You're right!" agreed Sue. "I love dinosaurs and the Tyrannosaurus is my favorite. He's so mean. I'll bring a model I made to our next club meeting."

When we left the dinosaur room, we walked
downstairs.

Sam still wanted to see the blue whale.

At the bottom of the stairs we heard a
funny noise.

"That noise sounds familiar," said Molly.

Molly was right!

The familiar noise was coming from Spot.

Spot was standing in the next room.

He was growling at a model of a humpback
whale.

"Spot! Come over here right now!" cried Molly.
"We've got to get him out of here," said Chris.
 Sue looked at Spot and asked, "How did you
      get in here anyway?"
Spot answered, *"Woof! Woof-woof-woof!"*
Molly explained:
      "Spot must have smelled those bones.
      He loves bones. He must have walked in
      through the service door. He sniffed
      his way right to here!"

Molly picked up Spot.

She tried to hide him under her jacket.

She walked quickly toward the nearest EXIT.

We all followed her.

Outside, Molly put Spot down on his four feet.

"Wow!" said Molly.

"Bow-wow!" said Spot.

# CHAPTER SIX

# FOR MEMBERS ONLY

There was a meeting the next day.

Scott started it off.

He banged two rocks together and said:

"Will this meeting please come to order!"

When everyone was quiet, Scott asked,
"Is there any old business?"

Sue answered. "I have some old business.
Here's the model of the Tyrannosaurus
that I made. Does anybody want to hear
how I made it?"

"I think your model's nice," said Roger, "but
I don't really want to hear how you made it."

"I agree," said Molly. "I'd rather *do*
something."

"I know what we can do," said Chris. "Spot,
come here. I need you."

Spot came.

Chris asked everyone to hide their eyes.

"Don't look!" Chris said.

Chris and Spot worked together.

Nobody knew what they were doing.

Every now and then Chris would say, "It'll just
be a few more minutes."

"Hurry up!" said Sue. "We're tired of waiting."

"Okay," said Chris. "Now you can open
    your eyes."
What do you think we saw?
There was Spot, looking just like a
Tyrannosaurus Rex!
Everybody started to laugh.
"You don't scare us!" shouted Scott.

"Let's play museum," said Molly.

"I can be a knight," said Chris.

"And I'll be the horse," said Sam.

"I'd like to be a brontosaurus," said Molly.
       "Who'd like to be my tail?"

"I would," said Sue. "I like to pretend."

When we stopped playing museum, Scott asked,
  "Is there any new business?"
Roger stood up. "I liked those buttons we got
  at the museum. I think we should make
  some."
"Buttons are hard to make," said Sam. "I have
  a better idea."
"Well, what is it?" asked Roger.
"Let's make membership cards," answered Sam.

"Cards are easy to make. All you need are markers and scissors—and some stiff paper," said Roger.

"I like Sam's idea," said Sue. "A membership card shows you belong."

"A card will fit right into my new wallet," said Molly. "I think—"

"I don't mean to interrupt," said Sam.

"Then don't," said Molly.

"But I want you to stop talking so we can get started," said Sam.

While she was working on her card, Molly asked, "Does anyone think other kids should be allowed to join the SMALL POTATOES?"

"I don't," said Roger.

"Now we're a small club," said Scott. "And I think we could use more members."

"But we can't fit more kids in this clubhouse," grumbled Roger.

"Well, we could have members who have their own clubhouses," said Scott.

Chris asked, "How can we do that?"

Scott answered. "They can make SMALL POTATOES membership cards at home. They can build their own clubhouses and have their own meetings."

"Gee, you're smart," said Sue. "We get members, but our small clubhouse doesn't get too crowded!"

"Let's vote about taking in new members,"
Roger said.

Somebody asked for a secret ballot.

After Roger had counted all the slips of paper,
he said, "Everybody voted 'Yes.' So other
kids are welcome to join the SMALL
POTATOES." (You can too!)

"Great," said Sue.

Molly said, "I move to adjourn this meeting."

"I second the motion," said Sam.

"Okay," said Roger. "Before we go, everyone
should know they're invited to the next
meeting of the SMALL POTATOES
CLUB. And don't forget to make your
membership cards!"

"See you next meeting!"

## SMALL POTATOES FUN

- Build a clubhouse with some friends. When you're all done, have a meeting.

- Since you now are a member of the SMALL POTATOES CLUB, make a membership card for yourself. You can copy the one below or invent your own.